For Simone and Nadia, their children, and their children's children . . .

—Mommy

IMPRINT
A part of Macmillan Publishing Group, LLC
175 Fifth Avenue, New York, NY 10010

ABOUT THIS BOOK
The text was set in Warnock Pro, and the display type is handlettered. The book was edited by Erin Stein
The production was supervised by Raymond Ernesto Colón, and the production editor was Dawn Ryan.

Honeysmoke: A Story of Finding Your Color. Text copyright © 2019 by Monique Fields.
Illustrations copyright © 2019 by Yesenia Moises. All rights reserved.
Printed in China by Hung Hing Off-set Printing Co. Ltd., Heshan City, Guangdong Province.

Library of Congress Cataloging-in-Publication Data is available.

ISBN 978-1-250-11582-9 (hardcover)

Our books may be purchased in bulk for promotional, educational, or business use. Please contact your local bookseller or the Macmillan
Corporate and Premium Sales Department at (800) 221-7945 ext. 5442 or by e-mail at MacmillanSpecialMarkets@macmillan.com.

Book design by Ellen Duda

Imprint logo designed by Amanda Spielman

First edition, 2019

1 3 5 7 9 10 8 6 4 2

mackids.com

Steal this book and forever color yourself cursed.

Honeysmoke

A story of finding your color.

MONIQUE FIELDS

illustrated by YESENIA MOISES

【Imprint】
MAKE YOUR MARK

NEW YORK

Simone wants a color.

She asks Mama, "Am I black or white?"
"Boo," Mama says, just like mamas do,
"a color is just a word."

She asks Daddy, "Am I black or white?"
"Well," Daddy says, just like daddies do, "you're a little bit of both."
But Simone still wants a color, one of her very own.

At lunch, she asks her friends, "What color am I?"

"You're black like me,"
one answers.

"No, you're white like me,"
says another.

"You could be one or
the other," a third says.

Simone stares at her feet. *No one* knows her color.

During recess Simone sways back and forth on a tire swing, and the black rubber stains her hands and clothes. It's not her color.

Inside the classroom, Simone creates a flower.
A drop of white glue kisses her skin. It's not her color.

Simone wants a color, one that shows who she is on the inside and the outside.

She snuggles with the bears in the reading corner. One is the color of chocolate, the other peanut butter.

She places their small hands on top of hers.
Neither chocolate nor peanut butter is her color.

She has two colored pencils. One brown, the other pink.
She draws a girl with one and colors her in with the other.

Simone isn't brown or pink.

Simone wants a color, one that tells *her* story.

She studies her parents during dinner.
She looks them up, then down.

Mama's skin reminds her of the honey
from the beehives at Grandma's house . . .

. . . and Daddy looks like the smoke
that billows from Grandpa's train.

Just before she climbs into bed,
Simone discovers her color.

"Mama," she says, "you're like honey
and just as sweet."
"Boo," she says, like mamas do,
"I'll never be as sweet as you are."

"And Daddy, you're the smoke.
You're the strongest man I know."
"Well," he says, like daddies do,
"you're the strongest girl I know."

Simone knows her color. She is . . .

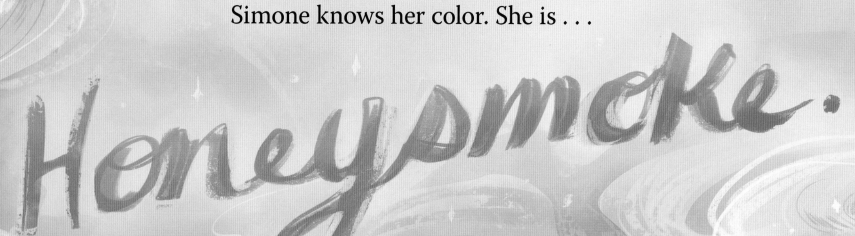

Honeysmoke.

HoneySmoke

The next day, she sees her color written in the clouds,
in the tree leaves, and on the grass,

and she writes it on her schoolwork,
on the classroom window, and in chalk on the playground.

Honey smoke

terracotta clay

sun quartz

Colors are words. Words are colors.
Discover your color word.

arctic pearl

bronze leaf

autumn gold

Write your color word here:

_____